TULSA CITY-COUNTY LIBRARY

P9-CBZ-152

W
,22

FEB - - 2022

POWER CODERS

FAKE NEWS AT NEWTON HIGH

AMANDA VINK

ILLUSTRATED BY JOEL GENNARI

PowerKiDS press™

New York

Published in 2021 by The Rosen Publishing Group, Inc.
29 East 21st Street, New York, NY 10010

Copyright © 2021 by The Rosen Publishing Group, Inc.

All rights reserved. No part of this book may be reproduced in any form without permission in writing from the publisher, except by a reviewer.

First Edition

Illustrator: Joel Grennari
Interior Layout: Tanya Dellaccio
Editorial Director: Greg Roza
Colorist: SirGryphon

Library of Congress Cataloging-in-Publication Data
Names: Vink, Amanda.
Title: Fake news at Newton High / Amanda Vink.
Description: New York : PowerKids Press, 2021. | Series: Power coders
Identifiers: ISBN 9781725307643 (pbk.) | ISBN 9781725307667 (library bound) |
ISBN 9781725307650 (6pack)
Subjects: LCSH: Journalism–Juvenile fiction. | Fake news–Juvenile fiction.
Classification: LCC PZ7.1.V564 Fa 2020 | DDC [F]–dc23

Manufactured in the United States of America

CPSIA Compliance Information: Batch CSPK20. For Further Information contact Rosen Publishing, New York, New York at 1-800-237-9932.

CONTENTS

Helping Out with the News . . 4

Something Fishy 9

The Moment of Truth. 15

Gotcha!. 21

Extra! Extra!. 30

HEY, GRACE!

WOOF!

HOW'S NEWTON HIGH NEWS?

HEY, CODERS....

I NEED TO COPYEDIT ALL THESE STORIES.

THEN I SEND THEM TO THE STUDENT WHO'S DOING THE DESIGN.

SHE'S WORKING ON HER COMPUTER AT HOME.

OK, NO PROBLEM.

MAYBE YOU CA[N] SPLIT UP AN[D] GIVE THE STOR[IES] A FINAL PROOF[F] AFTER I'M DO[NE] WITH THEM?

OF COURSE!

6

NEWTON FOOTBALL COACH TAKES BRIBE

According to leaked pic
Coach Jeremiah Jenkins
Newton High School too
as a bribe to keep star r
back Henry Lewis eligib
play so Lewis could ear
lege scholarship. On Tu
photographs surfaced sh
Jenkins accepting mone
Lewis. This apparent br
ethics could land the hig
coach of 30 years in pri
Lewis has been courted
number of college footb
but he's also had some academic issues in t

WOW.

THAT STINKS.

THERE'S SOMETHING WRONG HERE.

I KNOW IT....

AND I'M GOING TO FIGURE IT OUT.

WHAT ARE YOU GOING TO DO?

INVESTIGATE.

WE'RE IN.

WOOF!

YOU CAN TELL SOMETIMES WHEN A PHOTO HAS BEEN MANIPULATED.

SOMETIMES WHEN AN OBJECT IS EDITED IN, THE EDGES AROUND IT DON'T LOOK RIGHT.

ZOOM IN TO LOOK CLOSER!

YOU CAN ALSO LOOK AT THE LIGHT.

PAY SPECIAL ATTENTION TO THE DIRECTION THE SHADOWS FALL.

THIS PHOTO IS ACTUALLY REALLY BAD QUALITY.

THAT'S ANOTHER RED FLAG.

IT'S HARD TO TELL BECAUSE IT'S SO PIXELATED, BUT THE EDGES AROUND HENRY LOOK WEIRD.

DO YOU THINK THIS IS ENOUGH TO CONVINCE MARCY?

WE CAN TRY REVERSE SEARCHING THE IMAGE, TOO.

HOW DO YOU DO THAT?

YOU CAN DO IT FROM YOUR COMPUTER, PHONE, OR TABLET.

OPEN YOUR INTERNET BROWSER AND GO TO A SEARCH ENGINE FOR IMAGES.

UPLOAD YOUR OWN IMAGE AND CLICK SEARCH.

THE SEARCH ENGINE SPITS OUT ALL SIMILAR PHOTOS.

THEN YOU CAN DISCOVER THE SOURCE.

ON IT!

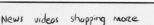

News videos shopping more

WHOA, THAT'S A LOT OF PICTURES TO SORT THROUGH!

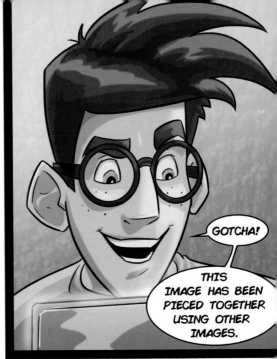

GOTCHA!

THIS IMAGE HAS BEEN PIECED TOGETHER USING OTHER IMAGES.

THE IMAGE OF COACH JENKINS AND HENRY WAS TAKEN FROM A PHOTO WHEN HEY WERE AT NATIONALS.

THE IMAGE OF THE CAMPUS IS FROM THE COLLEGE WEBSITE.

THE MONEY WAS NEVER THERE!

IT MUST'VE BEEN TAKEN FROM SOME OTHER PHOTOGRAPH.

I KNEW IT!

IT'S TOTALLY FAKE!

WE NEED TO TELL MARCY.

A LITTLE WHILE LATER...

AS YOU CAN SEE, THIS PHOTO HAS BEEN MANIPULATED.

THANK YOU FOR BRINGING THIS TO MY ATTENTION, GRACE.

THIS IS VERY SERIOUS.

YOU HAVE TO BE VERY SURE THAT A STORY IS TRUE, ESPECIALLY WHEN IT'S ABOUT SOMETHING SO SERIOUS.

DID YOU EVEN TALK TO THE COACH?

WHAT ABOUT THE PLAYER?

BUT PRINCIPAL GORDON... IF THIS STORY IS TRUE, WE NEED TO REPORT ON IT.

I FOUND DIFFERENT SOURCES.

JUST BECAUSE THE TIP WAS ANONYMOUS AND THE PHOTO IS FAKE, THAT DOESN'T MEAN THE FACTS ARE.

DID YOU ACTUALLY INTERVIEW ANYONE?

15

WHAT WERE YOUR SOURCES?

HERE, I'LL SHOW YOU.

WAIT, TAKE A LOOK AT THIS URL.

NEWTONGAZETTE.COM?

THAT'S THE LOCAL NEWSPAPER.

IT'S A RELIABLE SOURCE.

BUT THEY HAVEN'T RUN ANYTHING LIKE THAT!

I READ IT THIS MORNING AND I CHECKED THEIR WEBSITE.

IT ONLY LOOKS LIKE THE LOCAL NEWSPAPER!

WHAT?!

EWTON GAZETTE
Your News Now

DO YOU SEE HOW THERE ARE TWO ".COM"S?

THE ACTUAL DOMAIN NAME HERE IS "HEADLINE MANAGEMENT," AND A SUBDOMAIN HAS BEEN ADDED.

WHAT'S A SUBDOMAIN?

IT ALLOWS THE OWNER OF A WEBSITE TO PUT INFORMATION BEFORE THE DOMAIN, MR. CARR.

IN THIS CASE, IT'S ALLOWED THE OWNER TO BE TRICKY.

IT'S ALLOWED THEM TO MAKE THE URL LOOK LIKE IT'S COMING FROM THE LOCAL NEWSPAPER WHEN IT'S NOT.

17

WHAT ABOUT THESE OTHER SOURCES?

Gooble

(1) Facebook   Inbox (1)   Add shortcut

THIS ONE DOESN'T EVEN HAVE AN AUTHOR LISTED.

OH, GEEZ... SO MANY TYPOS!

A LOT OF FAKE NEWS SITES DON'T SPEND TIME CHECKING THEIR FACTS OR THEIR GRAMMAR.

NEWSPAPERS AND OTHER REPUTABLE SOURCES HIRE PEOPLE TO MAKE SURE THEIR CONTENT IS CLEAN.

GOTCHA!

JACK!!

HEY... IT LOOKS LIKE ALL THIS INFORMATION COMES FROM THE SAME PERSON.

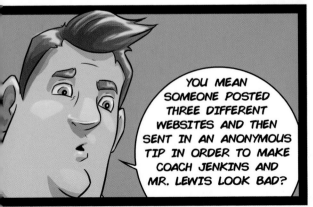

YOU MEAN SOMEONE POSTED THREE DIFFERENT WEBSITES AND THEN SENT IN AN ANONYMOUS TIP IN ORDER TO MAKE COACH JENKINS AND MR. LEWIS LOOK BAD?

BUT WHO WOULD DO SUCH A THING?

21

APPARENTLY, JOE SNYDER.

DID YOU JUST SAY "JOE SNYDER?"

YEAH... HE'S LISTED AS THE OWNER OF THIS WEBSITE.

MR. SNYDER USED TO GO TO NEWTON HIGH...

NEWTON HIGH SCHOOL YEARBOOK

MY MOM'S A LAWYER.

SHE SAYS THAT WHEN YOU PUBLISH SOMETHING THAT'S UNTRUE ABOUT SOMEONE ELSE, IT'S CALLED LIBEL.

YOU CAN GET IN TROUBLE FOR IT.

SO... THE COACH AND HENRY COULD TAKE HIM TO COURT?

HOW DOES THAT WORK?

MAYBE NO ONE WILL HAVE TO TAKE HIM TO COURT.

THE EMAIL IS LISTED, RIGHT?

I'LL SEND THE EMAIL.

AND I'M GOING TO MAKE SURE COACH JENKINS AND HENRY KNOW ABOUT THIS. GREAT JOB, GRACE.

EXCELLENT JOB, CODERS.

YOU REALLY SAVED US FROM A NASTY SITUATION.

MARCY, I THINK YOU NEED TO LEARN A LITTLE MORE FROM MR. HORNE AND THE SENIOR EDITORS BEFORE YOU'RE READY TO ACT AS MANAGING EDITOR AGAIN.

TAKE THIS AS A LEARNING EXPERIENCE.

AND THANK THE POWER CODERS!

YEP, RIGHT THERE.

MAYBE WE CAN SEND AN EMAIL ASKING HIM TO REMOVE THE LIBEL.

27

WHAT IS IT, PETER?

LET'S RUN A STORY ABOUT HOW TO SPOT FAKE NEWS.

PERFECT!

AND...

I HAVE THE PERFECT PICTURE!

I THINK THIS IS THE MOST POPULAR EDITION THE SCHOOL'S EVER HAD.

THANKS, PRINCIPAL GORDON!

I LOOKED THIS MORNING: IT LOOKS LIKE MR. SNYDER'S TAKEN DOWN ALL THE FAKE NEWSSITES.

YES!

SAY, HOW WOULD YOU KIDS FEEL ABOUT HOSTING A SEMINAR ABOUT HOW TO SPOT FAKE NEWS?

THERE'S SO MUCH FALSE INFORMATION OUT THERE THESE DAYS.

YEAH, I'M IN.

COOL!

LOOKS LIKE WE'LL NEED TO TAKE A LOT MORE PICTURES OF JACK FOR THAT SEMINAR.

BEAUTIFUL BEAUTIFUL

THE CAMERA LOVES YOU!

TRUE!

HE HAS MORE SOCIAL MEDIA FOLLOWERS THAN I DO!

WOOF